Moonville Ghost Stories and Haunts Along the Railway
ISBN-978-1-940087-61-0
Copyright © 2023
by Jannette Quackenbush
Let me help you find your scary place.

About the author: *Jannette Quackenbush is the author of 29 books, including Moonville: Its Past. Its Ghosts. Its Legends, Haunted Hiking Trails of the Appalachian Region, haunted Ohio, West Virginia, Pennsylvania, and New Orleans ghost guides. She is a veteran hiker, a seasoned backpacker, and a career author/naturalist/travel guide. She has provided tours and night hikes of Moonville and the surrounding communities.*

BackRoads Books
by 21 Crows
Jannette Quackenbush
Find Your Journey

Table of Contents

1876 map of the Moonville Rail Trail section of railway. Numbers show the area of the story and correspond with the ghost story in the Table of Contents.

The Place Called Moonville

When most imagine Moonville, they picture a sprawling town with many homes, buildings, and several streets filled with businesses. However, as far as having a population large enough, Moonville would hardly be called a town at all; there were only a couple of family homes in what would be a "town proper." Back when there were just dirt paths running through southeastern Ohio's Vinton County, two families, the Fergusons and Coes, lived on a certain section of land along the Raccoon Creek and Hewett Fork basin. Henry and Rhoda Ferguson were a farming family, and the family of Samuel and Emeline Coe had a mine and grist mill and were also lumber dealers, owning a remote sawmill.

It was Part of a Bigger Picture

But to talk about Moonville, you must include more than just this tiny place and the families living within. It was part of a much bigger picture. It was one small community but one deeply entwined with others nearby. And it all started with just those two families surrounded by other tiny communities desiring to interact commercially and socially. As it was difficult traveling and transporting products like coal to help fuel Big Sand Furnace and services toward Zaleski and Hope Furnace, Samuel Coe and Henry Ferguson asked the commissioners of Vinton County to make an extension of the road that already ran along Raccoon Creek from Bolin Mills on what is now State Route 50 (the route from Chillicothe, through McArthur, and then to Athens) to their properties connecting them to Hope and Hope Furnace (Big Sand Furnace) and Zaleski. After some discussion, the road was built and followed the path up and down the rugged and steep hills and beside Racoon Creek, connecting Ferguson and Coe's dirt thoroughfare to Big Sand Furnace.

At about the same time, the Marietta & Cincinnati Railroad, aware of the large pockets of rich coal in the region, began building tracks across southeastern Ohio. The railway ran between the properties, and trestles were constructed over the winding Raccoon Creek and Hewett Fork. The company gouged a tunnel through a particularly high hill on the Ferguson's land. They built a depot/train station on the Coe property. Then, the railway named the little community Moonville Station for the way the bright full moon hovered over this remote section of tracks and tunnel during certain times of the year. Small mining communities popped up along with Moonville, including Ingham Station (1.5 miles away), King Station (2.3 miles away), Mineral (3.6 miles away), and Luhrig (9 miles away).

These train tracks ran a much straighter line than the roadways following Raccoon Creek. They were also built above the flood zones on fairly level ground. Because of this ease of use, not only were the train tracks and trestles used by miners, sawmill workers, and iron furnace workers who would commute to work and sometimes to different towns where jobs were available, but they were also utilized heavily by families living in the mining communities from traveling to get food and sundries to visiting family members in outlying areas. The number of people walking the tracks made for a lot of accidents and deaths. As there was just a single set of tracks with eastward and westward bound trains utilizing them, it also made for many deadly train crashes. All those tragic deaths yielded a lot of ghosts. When the coal mining ended in the area, most of these remote communities were abandoned due to lack of work. However, with its heydays from the mid-1800s through the early 1940s, the railway had nearly a hundred years of heavy foot and train traffic. The last freight trains ran through Moonville in 1985. By 1988, over 30 miles of track were pulled. But as everyone knows, the ghosts from its past still remain.

Moonville and the Nearby Communities "The Bigger Picture"

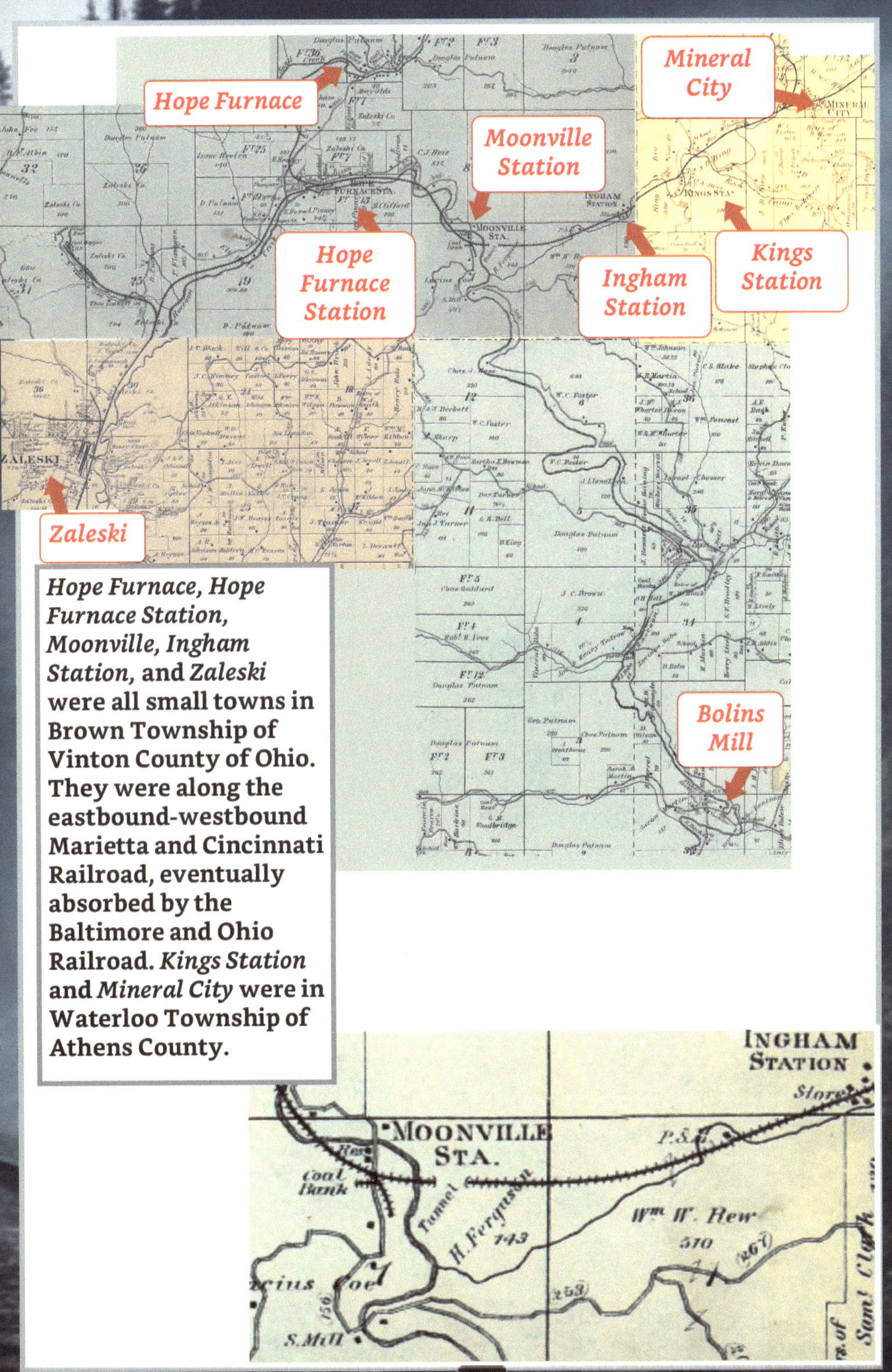

Hope Furnace, Hope Furnace Station, Moonville, Ingham Station, and Zaleski were all small towns in Brown Township of Vinton County of Ohio. They were along the eastbound-westbound Marietta and Cincinnati Railroad, eventually absorbed by the Baltimore and Ohio Railroad. Kings Station and Mineral City were in Waterloo Township of Athens County.

Zaleski

Zaleski was founded in the 1850s by Peter F. Zaleski, a native of Poland who offered large sums of money from his own funds and investors from his homeland to develop Zaleski Mining Company because of the rich local source of minerals. A town was laid out on purchased land with company houses for the workers to live in and a store to buy goods with company scrip. A home was even built for Zaleski, but he never set foot in the town. Foreseeing a bright future, saloons, stores, churches, schools, a brickyard, and a flour mill were built, which thrived for years. Along with the mines, there was a short-lived iron blast furnace. The town even offered three newspapers: the Zaleski Echo, Raccoon Navigator, and the Zaleski Herald. Its industries helped it become a prosperous village for many years along the Marietta & Cincinnati Railroad, even after the coal and iron industries began to wane. However, when fires destroyed its main source of employment for the community, the railroad shops, Zaleski lost its status as one of the most affluent communities in Vinton County. But not, of course, without leaving behind a ghost!

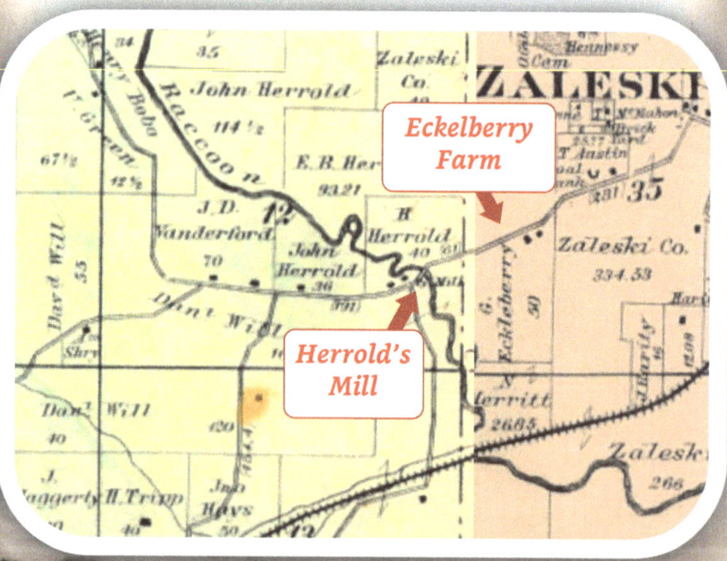

Zaleski in early 1900s, courtesy Vinton County Historical and Genealogical Society via Kenny Hayes

Zaleski in early 1900s, courtesy Vinton County Historical and Genealogical Society

WHITE THING OF ZALESKI

Powder Plant Road is a paved street leading out of Zaleski into the countryside. A bit less than a mile and a half from town and after crossing Raccoon Creek, it makes a sharp veer to the left. Those heading toward the county fairgrounds or the north side of McArthur can choose a shortcut and go straight, taking a more rugged road that eventually turns to gravel before ending at State Route 93.

At one time, the Vinton County Infirmary and its cemetery were settled on this path, and those in the community called it Infirmary Road. Farms were spread far apart along its route, and between the fields and meadows, there were patches of deep, dark forest.

Most people avoided this little stretch of road after dusk, especially the areas where the tree canopy was so thick that it blocked the moonlight. It had a ghost. Many reputable people witnessed it and said this shade followed them after dark. Alonzo Eckelberry, a local farmer, traveled the road from Zaleski on horseback one night in the late 1800s. About a mile out, just as he passed the old Herrold's Mill along Raccoon Creek and was in sight of a small house, he saw something white keeping pace beside him. The white thing sped up when the man hastened his horse with a tickle of his heels to ribs. When he slowed, the strange white thing also matched the pace.

As he passed the house, the specter jumped on the back of the man's horse. Startled, Eckelberry turned his horse around to race back to Zaleski. He could see the ghost perched atop the rear of his ride, but the horse appeared unaware. When he got to a slope called Shry Hill, the ghost jumped off. Eckelberry lost no time widening the expanse between himself and the horrifying apparition. And he refused, like many, to travel that route after dusk again!

Hope Furnace

Once called Big Sand Furnace, as it was along Big Sandy Run, Hope Furnace was one of 69 charcoal iron furnaces in the Hanging Rock Region, open from 1854 to 1874. It was used to smelt iron, extracting the impurities from the ore by melting. Fueling and running the furnace required hundreds of hired men who labored at the works, cutting timber or driving oxen teams to haul the ore. The charcoal (made by stacking and then burning cut wood) used to fuel the furnace was produced in the surrounding forest and then transported by oxen. From a nearby town called Hope Furnace Station, a horse would pull a railcar along a spur and up to the furnace, where laborers loaded the finished product, iron. Then, the railcar would return to the station. Buildings included a blacksmith shop, storage sheds, a wagon shop, and an office building. Across the road were houses for the several hundred workers who mined, cut timber, prepared the charcoal to fuel the furnace, and hauled the ore. There was even the largest school in the district, Hope Furnace School, with 70-100 students. Located on Irish Ridge Road, it is now long gone. There are few relics of Hope Furnace's past except its stone stack. Only foundation stones from the homes remain across the roadway where a pine grove now stands. Oh, and there are ghosts.

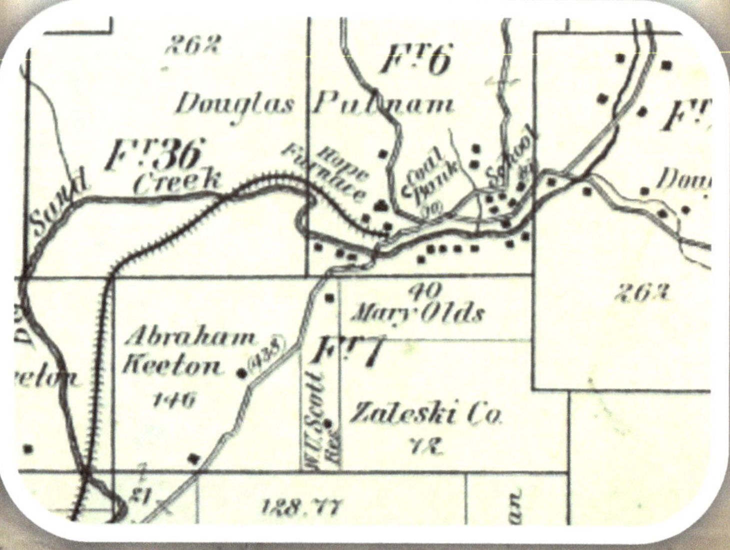

The background image is Buckeye Furnace in Jackson, Ohio. The image below is Hope Furnace in its heyday.

RETURN OF THE DEAD NIGHT WATCHMAN

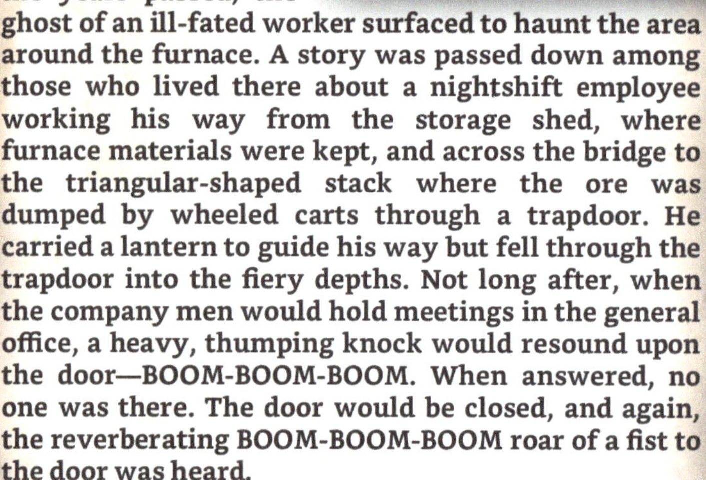

For 20 years, the charcoal iron industry flourished here, and as the years passed, the ghost of an ill-fated worker surfaced to haunt the area around the furnace. A story was passed down among those who lived there about a nightshift employee working his way from the storage shed, where furnace materials were kept, and across the bridge to the triangular-shaped stack where the ore was dumped by wheeled carts through a trapdoor. He carried a lantern to guide his way but fell through the trapdoor into the fiery depths. Not long after, when the company men would hold meetings in the general office, a heavy, thumping knock would resound upon the door—BOOM-BOOM-BOOM. When answered, no one was there. The door would be closed, and again, the reverberating BOOM-BOOM-BOOM roar of a fist to the door was heard.

Later, there were claims that a lantern light could be seen following the dead man's path—bobbing and winding its way from the outbuildings behind the stack, across the bridge, and to the furnace structure. The stack remained bare after the industry died away and the old buildings fell to ruin. Still, the ghost persists. If you look closely, you may catch a glimpse of the phantom lantern light dipping and weaving along its old path, heading along with the ghostly memories of the old furnace building and disappearing into the stack. And if you are standing by the parking lot or in the grassy bottomland, you may hear the BOOM-BOOM-BOOM of a ghostly hand knocking on a long-departed door.

When Hope Furnace was in operation, one of the workers fell down the stack at night with his lantern into the white hot ore. Later on people claimed that on some nights they'd see him on top of the stack with his lantern. At the big store at the furnace one night, some fellows inside heard a knock on the door and when they opened it no one was there. They thought it was him coming back—this happened several times—
As told by Mike Shea, Aug 16, 1961 to Bill Price

BURNT CABIN

Strange sounds sweep up from the deep forest along the Olds Hollow Trail at Lake Hope State Park and Zaleski State Forest. Their presence has been explained as this:

After the Civil War, two brothers working for the Hope Iron Furnace company as coalers lived in a small cabin near the furnace. The building burned to the ground one night, and the two died within. No one thought it could be foul play; it was mid-November and chilly. Those in the community assumed one or the other had started a fire to warm the thin-walled building by pouring into a tin bucket filled with wood some lantern oil made of camphene, a dangerous but cheap mixture of turpentine, alcohol, and camphor oil. It exploded. Not long after, those passing the area of the burnt cabin heard angry shouting issuing from the charred remains, but after a thorough search of the site, the curious found no source for the commotion.

Five years would pass, and in Tennessee, police arrested John Slavens for killing his nephew. He was tried and found guilty. As authorities were preparing to take him to prison, Slaven's wife confessed that she knew of two others the man had murdered. It was two young brothers who worked at a furnace in Ohio. Her husband had robbed them of their pay, murdered them, and then burned their cabin to hide his crimes. It was the two young men who lived at Hope Furnace. Upon hearing of the double murder, vigilantes broke down the prison doors and dragged Slavens to a tree. They tied a noose around his neck and hanged him until he died. Many years have passed, and nothing remains of the little burnt cabin in the woods but a few old foundation stones piled along with others. The charred remains of its walls have long decayed.

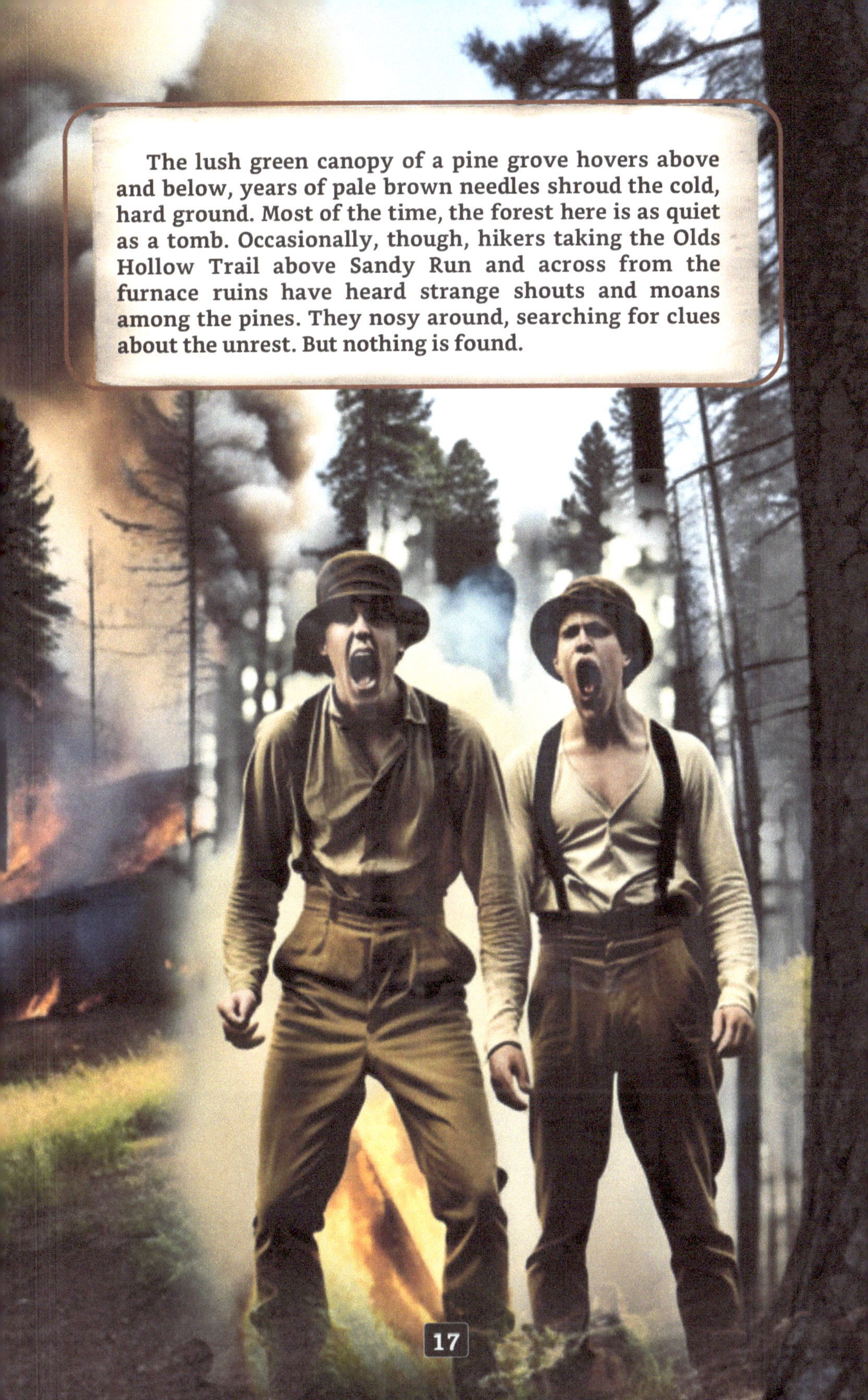

The lush green canopy of a pine grove hovers above and below, years of pale brown needles shroud the cold, hard ground. Most of the time, the forest here is as quiet as a tomb. Occasionally, though, hikers taking the Olds Hollow Trail above Sandy Run and across from the furnace ruins have heard strange shouts and moans among the pines. They nosy around, searching for clues about the unrest. But nothing is found.

Hope Furnace Station

Hope Furnace Station was another community along the Marietta and Cincinnati railway between Hope Furnace and Zaleski that blossomed when the Zaleski Company mined the land there. It is located on the long stretch of Shea Road between State Route 278/ Wheelabout Road and Hope-Moonville Road. Early residents laid the homes above the flood zone of Raccoon Creek near the railroad tracks from Zaleski to Moonville, near the spur track leading to Hope Furnace. The community was home to such families as the Sheas, Pinneys, Keetons, Lockharts, Fees, and Dunns. And a few spook lights that glowed at night.

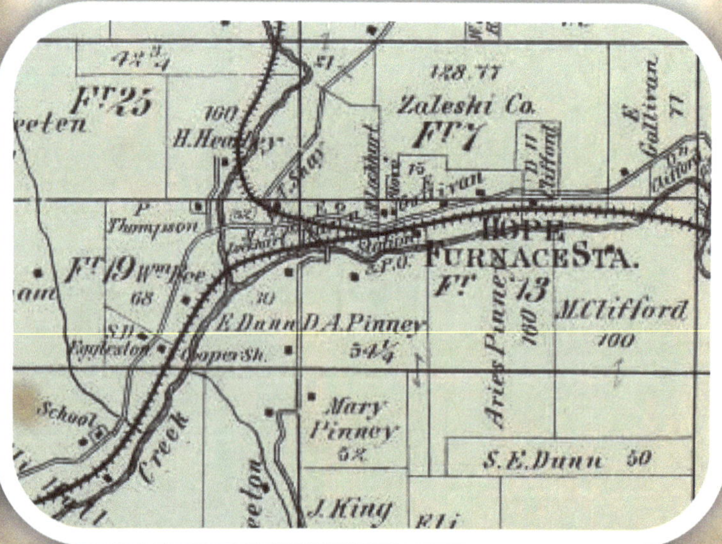

Hope Furnace Station today with Shea House, part of the Vinton County Parks.

Spook Lights of Hope Furnace Station

While the town of Hope Furnace was centered around the production of iron, Hope Furnace Station, a mile and a half away, was a coal mining, iron transport, and lumbering village along the railroad tracks. It was also where Matthew Lockhart (1842-1915), a carpenter by trade, set up his grocery store and saloon in the late 1800s and early 1900s.

There were a couple of murders at the Lockhart saloon, including the death of Jack Comer, killed by a man named Aaron with a scale weight. In addition, a bully named Baldie Keeton was thrown out of this saloon for his usual shenanigans and ended up dead on the railroad tracks that night.

People walking the railway here through town would see twinkling lights following them along the tracks—tiny orbs gleaming bright to faint over and over as if someone with two small lanterns was trying desperately to get their attention. Old-timers passed down the reason for this phenomenon, known as Spook Lights.

In the 1860s, a devoted family man and perfectionist tidied up his finances, completed all his business affairs, and gave his son a box with his family's valuable papers. He purchased powder and lead, loaded a musket, walked to the tracks going through Hope Furnace Station, and shot himself. When the twinkling lights began soon after, some believed that the man who had been so thorough in life forgot to do something before his death. He was frantically trying to tell those passing what he had neglected. But no one could determine what he was trying to divulge to them.

God Forsaken No Man's Land Between Hope Furnace Station and Moonville

Between Hope Furnace Station and Moonville, there was one mile of remote railroad with three trestles over Raccoon Creek and a series of "cuts," where workers had excavated straight through hillsides and left high cliff banks of earth and sandstone on either side. Engineers dreaded sections of track like this as these areas were prone to landslides and rockfalls as the exposed rock was on steep slopes, especially after hard rains. At any time, large stones barely clinging to the sand and dirt that held it could give way. And it did for more than one engineer, leaving a spirit that still walks those tracks.

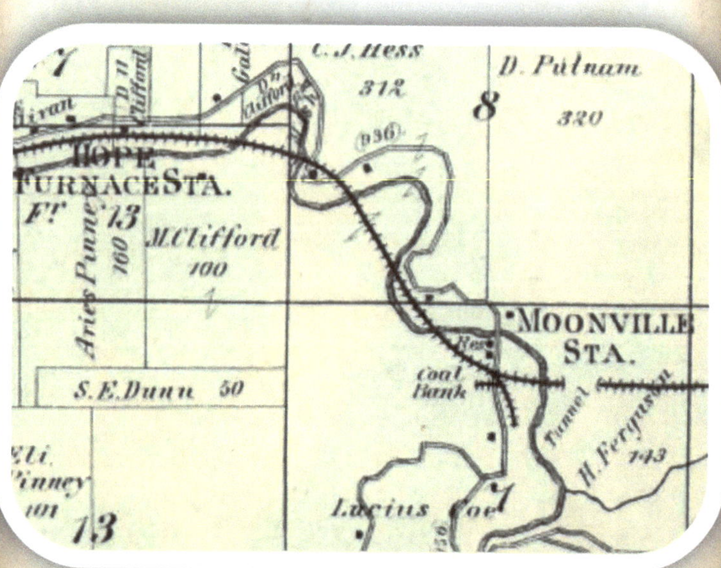

Wreck Area (taken from the east) about 6 days after the wreck that killed Red Landrum and crews had cleared much of the debris. You can still see rocks today from the fall. Image courtesy of the Estate of John R. Grabb.
The Marietta & Cincinnati railroad and its successor, the Baltimore & Ohio: a study of this once great route across Ohio, 1851-1988.
The infamous cut in the hill

LAST GOD-FORSAKEN RIDE OF RED LANDRUM

On December 26th, 1938, a 63 car Baltimore & Ohio freight train was careening down the lonely line of railroad tracks in a driving, icy rain between Moonville and Hope Furnace Station, about 6 miles east of Zaleski. It was a deserted run of railway, a God-forsaken mile after mile of nothing but a dark forest of no man's land. Few people lived along the abandoned route from the tiny village of Mineral to the quiet town of Zaleski; the booming coal and iron days were long gone. The wilderness had gobbled up any signs of civilization between the communities. Most townspeople had deserted their homes, the building's skeletal remains enduring now as bent and decaying wooden frames barely able to keep their stand against the winter winds. All that remained were a handful of abandoned cemeteries to leave evidence that a few souls had once lived there.

Impending winds as high as 35 miles per hour were heading towards McArthur, Allensville, and Athens. 54-year-old Charles "Red" Landrum was engineering the ill-fated train with no clue as the train sped around a bend that there had been a rockslide with a 100-ton boulder resting along the tracks until he caught it in his headlights too late. The train plowed full-speed straight into the enormous pile of rocks nearly 21 feet high, derailing the train, its second engine, and 12 of the 63 cars. The ensuing collision pinned Engineer Landrum in the cab with a broken leg, and he was scalded to death by the steam.

By December 28th, crews had cleared the track of wreckage, derailed cars, and stone. Yet, they did not remove the path of everything. The ghost of Engineer Landrum still haunts the railway in that no man's land between Hope Furnace Station and Moonville. Hikers have witnessed a contorted shadow wandering the cut in the hill where the wreck occurred, hear the ill-fated train's horn and piercing cry of wheels on rails, and a deep, mournful moan before it fades away to nothing.

Moonville

Moonville was never more than a tiny village of a couple of families, but it was a part of the bigger picture with other small outlying communities and their residents who passed along the railway tracks and through the town. It had a post office, a schoolhouse, a cemetery, a depot, a couple of Coe coal mines, their gristmill, and the sawmill down the road at another creek crossing. In Moonville proper, the two families were the Fergusons and the Coes. When driving along Hope Moonville Road just after the iron bridge and before crossing the area of the tracks, the two-story Coe home and outbuildings were on the right. Nearby was a depot. Across the dirt road, the Fergusons lived and farmed the land. Neighbors were few and far between. Their only remnants are a handful of foundation stones, old wells, and rusted fencing. When the railway plowed through and the coal mines began to thrive, the route through this section of Ohio was dreaded by engineers because of its remoteness. It was not just that only one set of tracks were shared by eastbound and westbound trains, and there were more than a few head-on crashes. Nor was it the many rock falls in the steep cuts between hills for the tracks. Most wanted to avoid the four miles between Hope Furnace Station and Kings Station's tunnel after dusk because there were suspicions among more than a few that ghosts haunted the tracks.

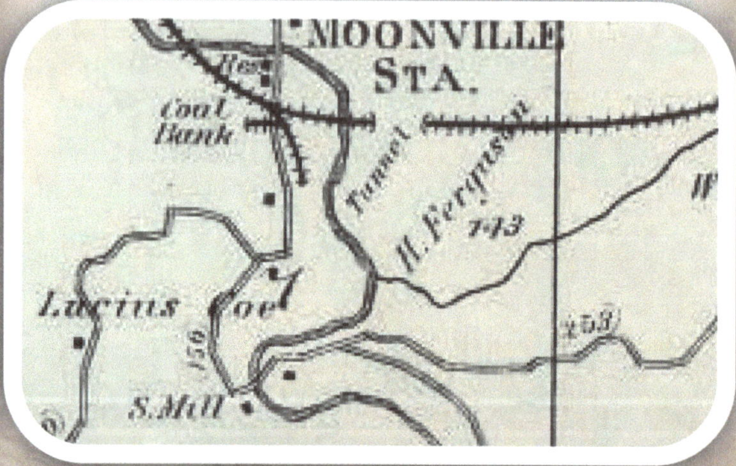

OONVILLE

The Coes

Around the 1830s, Samuel (1813 – 1883) and Emaline (1817-1895) Coe moved to the area that later became Moonville with their family and built a grist mill close to Moonville proper and a steam sawmill down the road from the cemetery, both on Raccoon Creek. Coe transported his logs along the creek until around 1858 when he and neighbor Henry Ferguson petitioned the county for a road running from the mill on Raccoon Creek through Moonville, Big Sand Station (Hope Furnace Station), and to Big Sand Furnace (Hope Furnace) to allow area businesses and the entire outlying communities to prosper. The town would certainly grow and flourish, as did many, with the mining of coal there and the railway running through it.

Aug. 5, 1858.—ts—4d50.

Road Notice.

NOTICE is hereby given that a petition will be presented to the Commissioners of Vinton County, Ohio, at their next session, for an order to open a road in Brown Township, in said county, commencing at Coe's Mill on Raccoon Creek, thence by way of Moonville and the residence of Alonzo Ferguson, to Big Sand Furnace, being an extension of the county road leading from Boland's Mill, on said creek to Coe's Mill.
H. FERGUSON,
and other citizens of Brown Township.
July 29.—4w

Mr. Samuel Coe, about a quarter of a mile west of Moonville, opened a new coal mine on the banks of Raccoon, about 20 feet above high water mark, being the Nelsonville seam—about 5½ feet thick.— The coal can be dumped into a boat on Raccoon, with no other cost than that of mining.

The Zaleski Company have opened a ___ mile west of ___

Coal Miners Wanted.

100 MEN can find steady employment for the winter at the **Moonville Coal Mines**, 15 miles west of Athens.
G. A. & R. P. ARMES & Co.
Moonville, Nov. 26, 1856—4w47

CANDIES, Toys and Nuts, of various kinds, for sale by
J. B. WILKIN.

The First Coes in Moonville

First Generation in Moonville

Samuel Coe 1813–1883

Spouse: Emaline Newcomb Coe 1817–1895 (m. 1836)

Children in Household:

George Delos Coe 1837-1911 (Age 73, Buried in California)

Thomas Seymoure Coe 1839–1841 (Age 2, Buried in Moonville)

Mary Jane Coe Higgins 1842–1896 (Age 53, Buried in West Virginia)

William Clifton Coe 1844–1899 (Age 54, Buried in Moonville)

Elizabeth Coe 1846–1846 (Age 1, Buried in Moonville)

Preston Coe 1847–1865 (Age 17, Buried in Moonville)

Romaine Coe 1848–1932 (Age 84, Buried in Washington State)

Emma Bliss Coe Linton 1854–1920 (Age 66, Buried in New Marshfield, Ohio)

Martha Ellen Coe 1855–1863 (Age 8, Buried in Moonville)

Oscar Ebenezer Coe 1858–1906 (Age 48, Buried in Chillicothe, Ohio)

Adelaide "Addie" Clara Coe Skinner 1860–1947 (Age 86, Buried in Wisconsin) Moonville Schoolteacher

Martha "Mattie" Coe (1864-?) Moonville Schoolteacher

Second Generation in Moonville

William Clifton (Cliff) Coe   1844– 1899

Spouses: Allie Prudence Keeton Bond

1866–1935 (m. 1887)

Lovisa Jane Porter Coe 1843–1885

Children in Household:

Jacob L. Coe 1868–1869 (Age 10 months, Buried in Moonville)

Francis Romaine Coe 1869–1955 (Age 85, Buried in Keeton Cemetery)

Baby Coe 1872–1873 (Age 1 month, Buried in Moonville)

Cora M Coe Wey 1874-?

Grace Marie Coe Smith 1878–1916 (Age 37, Buried in Canada)

William P Coe 1884–1884 (Age less than a year, Buried in Moonville)

Mabel Gertrude Coe Douglas 1889–1972 (Age 83, Buried in Oregon) Note: Mabel was a granddaughter living in the home: (father: William Clifton Coe 1844 – 1899

Mother: Alice P. Keeton 1866 - 1935

The Coe Home. One of the last house standing at Moonville was built by Samuel Coe, one of the first settlers to the area. The Coes were originally from Connecticut. Image: Vinton County Historical Society and Neil Dearth, great-great grandson of Samuel Coe.

Oscar Coe—1905-06. and his sister, Bernice Coe (Dearth), on the front porch of the Coe home in Moonville. Image: Neil Dearth (his mother is to the left) and Vinton County Historical and Genealogical Society.

The location of the depot, store, post office, and main Coe home stood in Moonville on the right side of Moonville Road between the bridge (above) and the railroad tracks.

39.309617, -82.324695 to
39.308655, -82.324716

The Fergusons

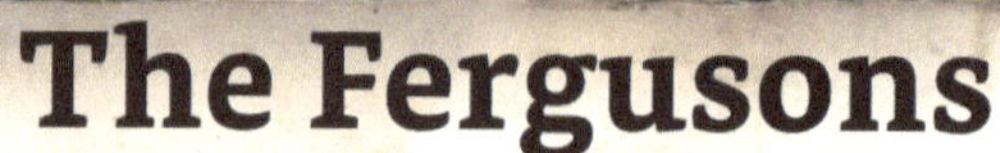

The Henry and Rhoda Ferguson family settled in Vinton County early, farming their land across the dirt road from the Coes. Family members also worked for the iron furnaces, local coal mines, and railway. Hikers can walk through part of the Ferguson property, now Ohio Division of Forestry land. The seasonal and unmaintained trail is a small pull-off before the iron bridge on Hope-Moonville Road. Many old foundation stones and a deep, brick-walled well still exist. Those with a keen eye may discover a few old still-house barrels near the tunnel; it was rumored that there were more than just spectral spirits a-brewing in Moonville—somebody made whiskey up there during the 1920s prohibition period, and folks visited quite often to buy the drink.

The First Fergusons in Moonville

First Generation in Moonville

Henry Ferguson 1791–1871
Spouse: Rhoda Goodrich Churchill 1806-1879

Children in Household:

William Ferguson 1847 - 1909 Buried in Buchtel, Ohio
Cordelia Ferguson 1842–1912 (Buried in Indiana)
Joseph Clark (Rhoda's son from first marriage) 1830-?

Hiking the rugged path to the old Ferguson property

Moonville Tunnel in years past when the train still ran through it. The Ferguson property would be on the left and right in the picture. Images courtesy: Lori Grupenhoff.

Moonville School

At the turn on the hill (left side) heading along the dirt road to the Moonville Cemetery, the one-room Moonville Schoolhouse once overlooked Raccoon Creek on a small bluff. Only a few foundation stones remain of the building. Some teachers included Adelaide "Addie" Coe, Martha "Martie" Coe, and Effie Stephenson Ward.

Moonville Cemetery

The town and surrounding area may never have been large, but life expectancy was shorter in rural areas without a local doctor and medicine nearby. Being along the railroad, where fast-moving trains shared the tracks with miners commuting to work and folks traveling from town to town to visit family or obtain groceries and sundry items, also made for more than a few deaths. The area seemed to have more than its share of tragedies, and it shows in the small cemetery just up a twisty gravel road because it seems to burst with graves from both the young and old of the community. If lung fever or cholera did not get them, the railroad running through town took its share of folks. Although few gravestones remain, those who look hard can see markings in the hard-packed soil where monuments to the dead, either wood or stone, once laid.

Known Burials

***Coe, Samuel** (7/20/1813 - 4/ 21/1883)
Spouse:
***Coe, Emaline Newcomb** (11/4/1817-11/5/1895)

Children of Samuel and Emaline Coe buried at Moonville:

***Coe, Martha Ellen** (8/20/1855-9/3/1863)
Inscription: I want to be an angel and with the angel stand. A crown upon my forehead and a harp within my hand.
***Coe, Thomas Seymour** (1839-1841)
***Coe, Elizabeth Coe** (1846–1846)

Coe, Preston
(3/22/1847 - 2/28/1865)
Son of Samuel and Emaline Coe
Inscription: 17y 11m 6d
Son of Samule & Linaline Coe

***Coe, William Clifton "Cliff"**
(6/30/1844– 4/28/1899)
Died of a heart attack while holding a child (Ruth) in the Moonville Depot.
Spouse: Lovisa Coe

***Coe, Lovisa Jane Porter** (12/8/1843 - 2/6/ 1885)
Died of consumption.
Spouse: Cliff Coe
Children of Cliff and Lovisa buried at Moonville:
***Coe, Jacob L.** (1868 - 3/5/1869)
***Coe, Baby** (1872-1873) Died of croup
***Coe, William P.** (1884 - 10/20/1884)

***Coe, Wellington C.**   (Brother of Samuel Coe)
(3/10/1824 - 2/28/1887)
Died from pneumonia (lung fever).
Inscription: Co C, 30th O.V.I. Civil War Veteran

***Jones, Benjamin Thomas**
(May 22, 1832 - February 24, 1912)
Spouse:
***Jones, Rachel Josephine Stilwell**
(June 12, 1842 - April 1, 1914)
Children of Benjamin and Rachel buried at Moonville:
***Jones, Louzanna M.**   (1862- 9/14/1865)
 Inscription: 3 years 15 days Daughter of B. & R. Jones

***Ferguson, Charlie** (October 1829 - 1902) brother of Henry Ferguson Struck by a train when crossing the tracks in Moonville.

***Joiner**, Infant Unknown

***Jones, Eber Eugene**
(12/3/1875- 6/30/1876)
Inscription: Asleep in Jesus

***Jones, Ideliae**
(6/5/1874 - 7/15/1874)
Inscription: Asleep in Jesus

***Mace, Grace** (1877 - 8/24/1877) Daughter of Hiram and Adeline Scott Mace

***Mace, James** (1833– 8/24/1899) Grandfather of Frank Mace. Spouse: Martha Elizabeth Mace.

***Ross, Jerry (Jeremiah)** (1841 - unknown died before 1880 but was still alive in 1860 census at age 20) Uncle of Billy Ross and Brother of Newton Ross

***Stilwell, Matilda** (1798 - 3/17/1870) (Mother of William and Isaiah Jr. Stilwell.) Spouse: Isaiah Stilwell

***Stilwell, William**
(9/20/1827 - 5/5/1876)
***Stilwell, Sarah Ann Lentner**
(10/24/1830 - 8/ 21/1905)
***William Stilwell** (1827 - 1876)
 ***Stilwell, Albert** (1896 - 1900) Age 4 -Choked to death on a .22 cartridge Lived at the head of Wolf Pen Hollow. Child of Sarah Elizabeth Bowman and Isaiah Dallas Stilwell
 ***Stilwell, Bessie Viola** (9/14/1905–10/2/1910) Daughter of Frank and Cordelia Stilwell   Age 6. Hot cup of coffee spilled down her back.
 ***Thorn, Constantine** (8/16/1863-10/11/1863) Son of F.M. and S. Thorn. Aged 2 months, 26 days.

THE GHOST OF MOONVILLE

In the 1800s in southeastern Ohio, there were small mining communities along the Marietta & Cincinnati Railroad between Zaleski and Athens. Among them was Moonville, a settlement along the Raccoon Creek with two families living in the town proper. The Fergusons were farmers and railway workers, and the Coes had a sawmill, gristmill, train station/depot, and mine. Also, along the tracks, telegraph lines ran from train station to train station so that dispatchers could communicate with each other. Their interactions were very important as the railroad had only one set of tracks, and trains traveled in both an eastward and westward direction. The dispatcher's job was to monitor and control the signals so engineers knew when to pull off the tracks if there was a rockfall on the rails or to let an oncoming train pass. Most of the time, the system worked quite well. Sometimes, however, it failed.

Theodore Lawhead was an engineer for the Marietta & Cincinnati Railroad. On one November night in 1880, while Engineer Lawhead was heading through southern Ohio, the dispatch failed to notify his eastbound train of the westbound's route and time. The trains collided near Moonville Tunnel, and Lawhead and his fireman died instantly. After the wreck, many trainmen feared going along that stretch of the railroad. They said they would see the flicker of candlelight when they came along a certain section of the tracks near the tunnel in Moonville where Lawhead died. As they got closer and slowed, believing that someone was signaling an emergency ahead, a white-robed figure appeared carrying a lantern, floating down the hillside with wide bulging red eyes, and a halo of tiny lights flickering around its head. Then it would disappear!

THE BRAKEMAN'S WHISKEY BOTTLE

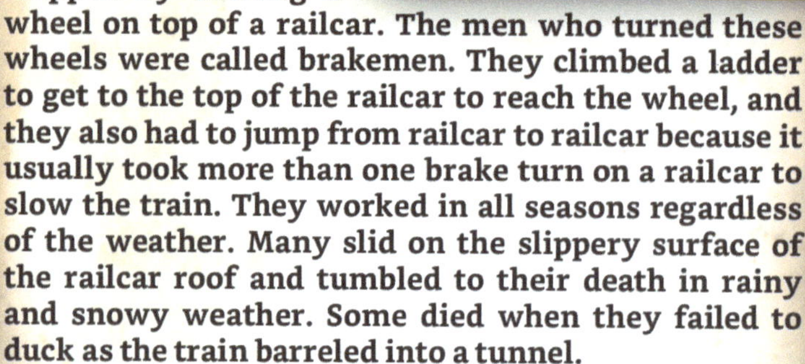

In the early days of the railroad, trains were slowed or stopped by turning a wheel on top of a railcar. The men who turned these wheels were called brakemen. They climbed a ladder to get to the top of the railcar to reach the wheel, and they also had to jump from railcar to railcar because it usually took more than one brake turn on a railcar to slow the train. They worked in all seasons regardless of the weather. Many slid on the slippery surface of the railcar roof and tumbled to their death in rainy and snowy weather. Some died when they failed to duck as the train barreled into a tunnel.

The brakeman's job was stressful and many turned to drinking. One such brakeman was going along the track from Zaleski to Moonville one night. He held a bottle of whiskey in his hand, which he sipped along the way. The more he walked, the more he sipped. The more he sipped, the drunker he got. The drunker he got, the more tired he began to feel until, at some point, he decided to take a nap. All would be fine except for three things: he used the rails as a pillow, the track as a bed, and sometime during the night, a train came along and took off his head. His head bounced in one direction, over the track and down into a small ravine where Raccoon Creek was flowing heavily. His body flopped to the other side of the path and lay neatly secreted into the brush. The bottle spun around in the center of the tracks and then stopped without sloshing out much whiskey at all.

The next morning, a miner heading from Moonville to Zaleski came across the bottle of whiskey lying on the tracks. "What a find!" he exclaimed, reaching down to pick up his prize. As his fingers touched the glass, he heard a raspy voice call out, "That's mine!"

The miner's head shot up. He looked left to right but could not find the source of the voice. Then his eyes dropped to the bed of the tracks, and he saw little specks of blood and followed them up and over the rail and to the area where the train track ballast stones stopped. He reached out, parted the thick brush, and there before him was the corpse of the brakeman. But there was no head, and it was never found. The whiskey bottle was largely forgotten. It lay there for years in the center of the tracks because anyone who reached down to pick it up never let it stay in their grasp for long as they were nearly scared to death when the ghost of the brakeman called out, "That's mine!"

LAVENDER LADY

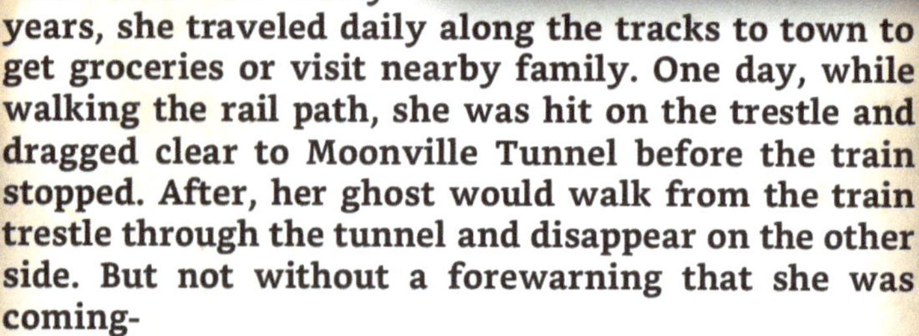

An old woman lived in a tidy little house a little ways from Moonville. For many years, she traveled daily along the tracks to town to get groceries or visit nearby family. One day, while walking the rail path, she was hit on the trestle and dragged clear to Moonville Tunnel before the train stopped. After, her ghost would walk from the train trestle through the tunnel and disappear on the other side. But not without a forewarning that she was coming-

In the 1800s, people bathed less often than nowadays, perhaps once or twice a month. Instead, they applied fragrances to cover up unsavory scents. These fragrances were not usually applied directly to the skin as they are today. Instead, women blotted rose, lemon, or lavender botanicals on kerchiefs, stuffed them beneath their clothing, or sprinkled the scents on their skin and garments. Older folks used these same healing oils as a rubbing salve to remedy aches and pains. Some believe that lavender was the oil the old woman had used as a perfume or massaged on her aching elbows or knees that fateful day before taking her last trip to town. Before her ghost passed, startled bystanders would catch the heavy scent of lavender wafting in the air. And some still do!

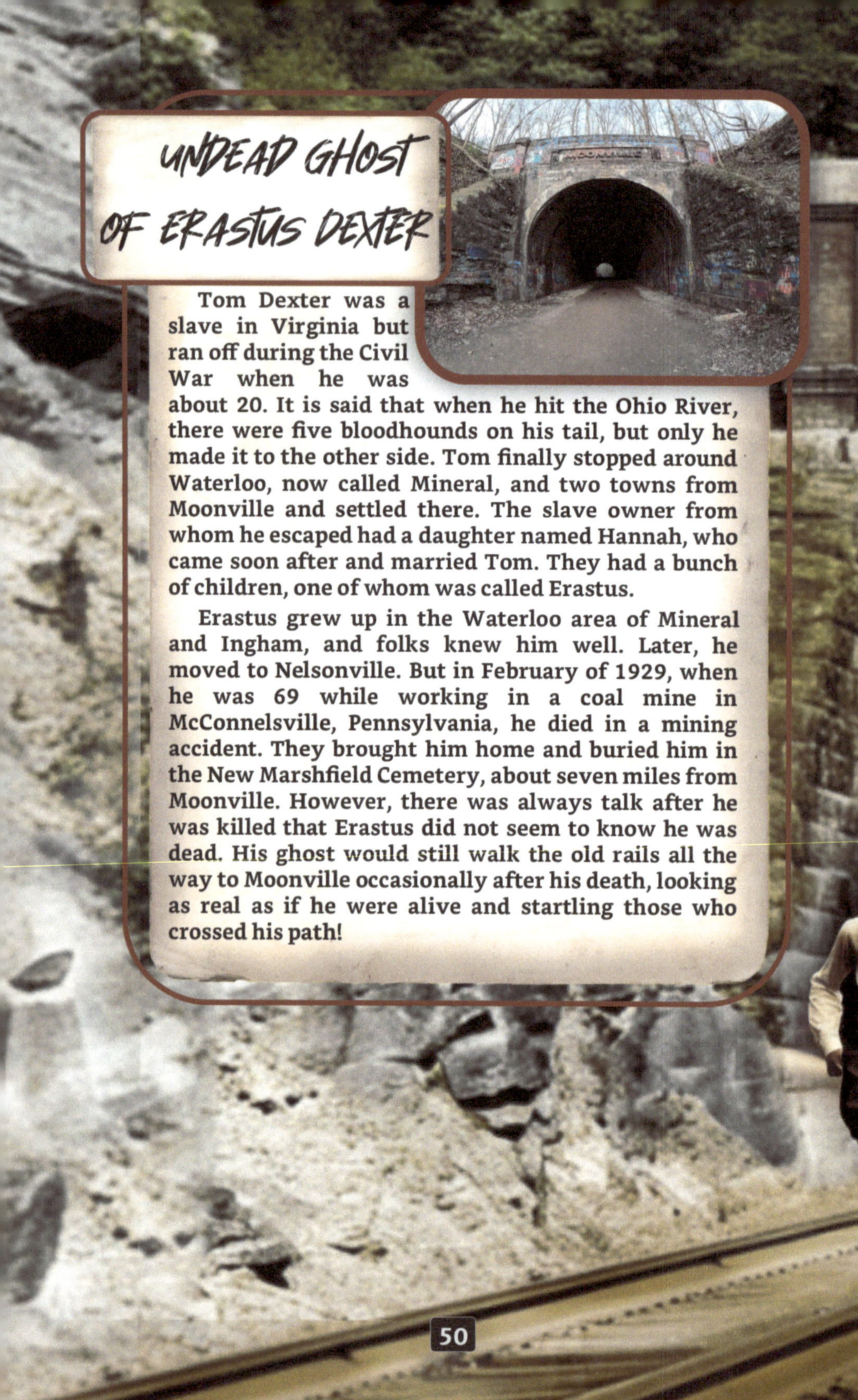

UNDEAD GHOST OF ERASTUS DEXTER

Tom Dexter was a slave in Virginia but ran off during the Civil War when he was about 20. It is said that when he hit the Ohio River, there were five bloodhounds on his tail, but only he made it to the other side. Tom finally stopped around Waterloo, now called Mineral, and two towns from Moonville and settled there. The slave owner from whom he escaped had a daughter named Hannah, who came soon after and married Tom. They had a bunch of children, one of whom was called Erastus.

Erastus grew up in the Waterloo area of Mineral and Ingham, and folks knew him well. Later, he moved to Nelsonville. But in February of 1929, when he was 69 while working in a coal mine in McConnelsville, Pennsylvania, he died in a mining accident. They brought him home and buried him in the New Marshfield Cemetery, about seven miles from Moonville. However, there was always talk after he was killed that Erastus did not seem to know he was dead. His ghost would still walk the old rails all the way to Moonville occasionally after his death, looking as real as if he were alive and startling those who crossed his path!

MOONVILLE

THE BULLY

The Keetons were one of the prominent founding families of the Hope Furnace and Hope Furnace Station communities, owning much of the farmland there, including the land where the Hope Iron Furnace was built. Several generations of large farming families had extended into the outlying area and were well-liked. But every family has its black sheep, one that gains notoriety for the deeds they have done. David "Baldie" Keeton was just that, a farmer who lived near Hope Furnace Station.

Baldie was 65 years old in 1886. a huge hulking beast of a man, and still as stalwart as he had been in his younger years. He was a bully who would pick up tiny rocks and toss them at those around him just to irritate them into a fight, especially when he got drunk. And Baldie liked to drink a lot. He was notorious for getting soused, picking a fight with the littlest man in the room, and giving him a bear hug so hard that the other man could not breathe. Eventually, it would knock this smaller rival out.

When those in the mining towns saw Baldie walking the tracks from Zaleski to Ingham Station, they avoided him. He was also the local tax collector, which led to many hard feelings in the community when he banged on folks' doors to collect their fees. If they could not pay, he dragged them to court. Few in the county liked Baldie Keeton, and Baldie Keeton did not like anyone in return.

On Saturday evening of June 26, 1886, Baldie stopped off at a bar after returning from a late-night court appearance in Zaleski. He got drunk, started a fight, and was escorted from the property. Baldie did not go home that night, and his wife, assuming that he had gotten drunk and slept it off with nearby family, did not contact anyone for a day. After some time, she sent out a party to search for him, and they found his mangled corpse on the tracks.

The coroner stated Baldie died from getting hit by a train, and most newspapers printed the aged man had fallen asleep on the tracks because of the late-night court case. However, everyone from Hope Furnace to Mineral believed he was dead long before the first, second, and third train hit him, and they were glad for it even if they did not say it aloud. After, mothers in the vicinity would warn their children not to go near the tracks and not stay out after dark. If they did, old Baldie Keeton might get them. His ghost was often seen hunched over and shuffling drunkenly along the railroad between Zaleski and Moonville Tunnel, grumbling to himself as if still walking the tracks to collect those past-due taxes or perhaps seek out someone smaller to bully. He is also spotted above the tunnel, standing still and solitary and known to throw rocks and pebbles at those walking beneath.

Ingham Station

Ingham Station was created when the Marietta & Cincinnati Railroad ran through, and small mining communities popped up. It was founded by two brothers named Ingham. It had a school, several homes, a general store, a station, and mines across the tracks in Bear Hollow in its heyday. By 1914, most in town had left when the mines closed a few years earlier. No roads ran to Ingham and this area remained a remote pocket few visited. However, those who did occasionally heard or saw a ghost train along the old tracks.

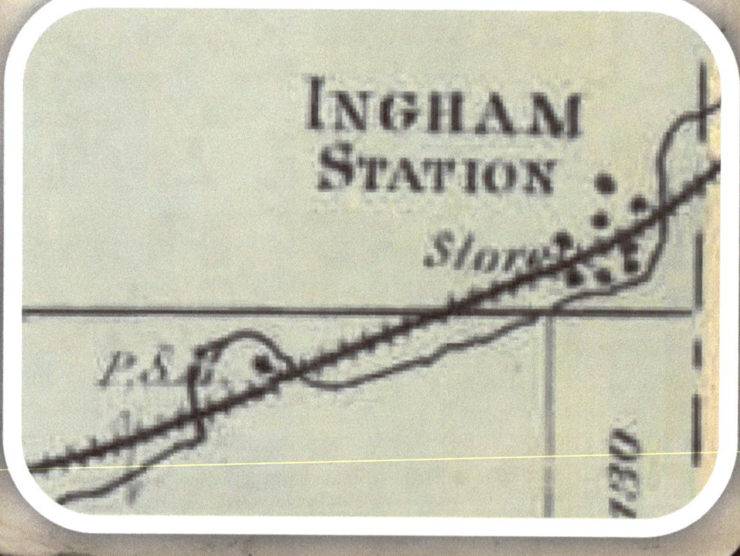

924

THE LOST HAND

Allen Allbaugh and his brother worked as coal miners and traveled back and forth between Zaleski and Luhrig just outside Athens. Instead of walking the one-way trip of nine miles each day, they would wait for the blow of the train's whistle, and then, as it slowed within the town limits, the two would hitch a ride. One evening in the late summer of 1907, they got off work early after working in Zaleski and decided to stop at a bar. As it was payday, Allen bought a bottle of whiskey, and the two settled for a drink. However, only moments later, they heard the holler of the train as it barreled down the tracks. The Baltimore & Ohio rolling through this evening was early! Both dashed outside and toward the railway to hop on for a free ride, Allen still holding his whiskey bottle tight in his fist.

When the train got to Luhrig, Allen's brother jumped off, but Allen was nowhere to be found. Nobody was that worried at first, as Allen's foot had been mashed by a fall of coal at a mine in Luhrig several years earlier. He walked with a peculiar limp and had, in the past, had difficulty catching the train as his injury slowed him down. Sometime later, though, two men walking the tracks along Hewitt Fork near Ingham Station and Bear Hollow smelled something ghastly in the brush. Thinking it was a dead deer, they parted the grasses. However, it was the badly decomposed corpse of Allen Allbaugh, and he was missing a hand. Allen's body was taken home and placed into a plain wooden coffin. A grave was dug in the dirt, and he was buried deep and properly, but soon after, someone else traveling through Moonville Tunnel found his hand lying in some brush just outside, along with shards of glass.

Most presumed that Allen caught the tail end of the train that fateful day it was early. But muddled from the booze and hanging on with one hand to the side of the car, he had teetered to one side. The hand holding the bottle of whiskey had been swept out and was chopped off by the tunnel wall.

Somebody must not have buried Allen's hand with the rest of his body, or maybe not as deep. Those walking the tracks near Ingham Station began seeing a man limping along the rails appearing confused. When they paused to address him, he raised his arm to show nothing more than a stub where his hand used to be before disappearing. Everyone knew it was the ghost of Allen Allbaugh. He was searching for his hand.

King Station & Mineral City

When the railroad was built, many then-isolated landowners gave the railway right of way across their property, knowing that a train passing through was a good investment. It connected them with other communities, and property owners could profit from the resources their land provided. The King family owned land along the train route, opened profitable mines on their property, and cashed in on the railway this way. A town was formed, run mainly by Silas King, with a schoolhouse, store, post office, and housing for 50 to 60 people. One of the Kings, Doc, had a saloon/store in his home. It also has a wooden tunnel down the track that is still accessible along the rail trail.

A mile down the tracks from King Station, another town that popped up in the coal mine years was Waterloo, also known as Mineral City. Coal mining was not the only thing these two towns had in common; they shared a ghost!

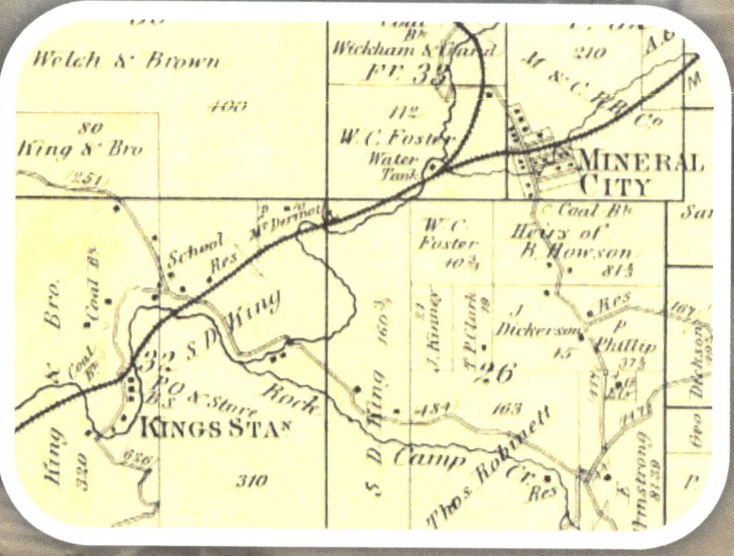

ERNEST KEETON RUNS FROM A GHOST

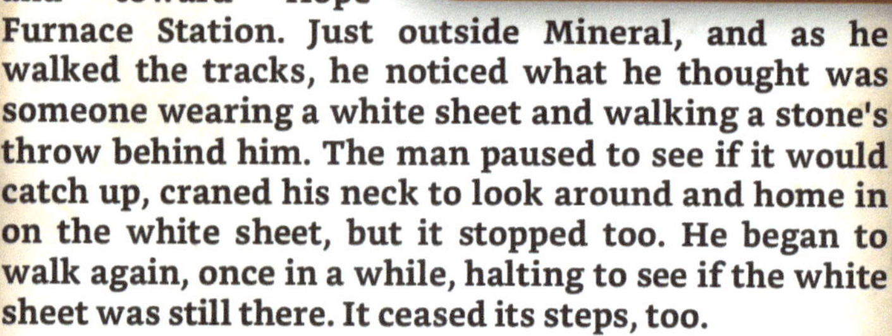

One night, Ernest Keeton was heading through Mineral City and toward Hope Furnace Station. Just outside Mineral, and as he walked the tracks, he noticed what he thought was someone wearing a white sheet and walking a stone's throw behind him. The man paused to see if it would catch up, craned his neck to look around and home in on the white sheet, but it stopped too. He began to walk again, once in a while, halting to see if the white sheet was still there. It ceased its steps, too.

Spooked, Ernest began to quicken his pace only to find that the faster he walked, the quicker the white figure walked. The white sheet kept this pace until Ernest realized it had sped up so that it was right on the opposite end of the ties as he was. Yet even though it was directly beside him, it was not making a sound! So unnerved was Ernest that he decided to run. He ran past King Station, Ingham Station, Bear Hollow, a long stretch of nothing but deep forest, and all the way to Moonville with that white thing racing and floating right next to him the entire time. As he sprinted into Moonville Tunnel, choking for breath, it dipped down a ravine into the woods and disappeared.

EiGHT FOOT GHOST

Between Mineral and Moonville were swampy marshlands and no roads from one town to the next. People had no choice

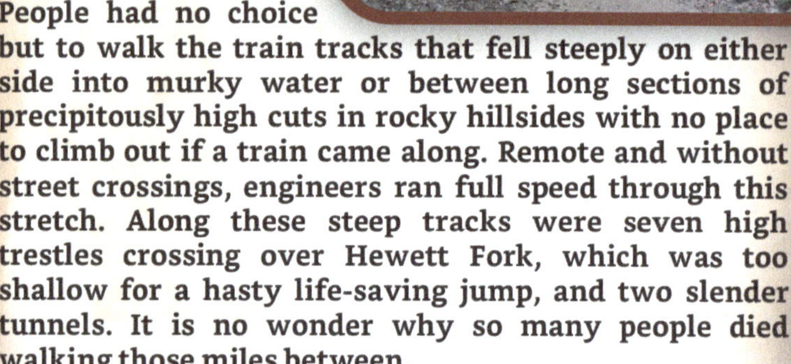

but to walk the train tracks that fell steeply on either side into murky water or between long sections of precipitously high cuts in rocky hillsides with no place to climb out if a train came along. Remote and without street crossings, engineers ran full speed through this stretch. Along these steep tracks were seven high trestles crossing over Hewett Fork, which was too shallow for a hasty life-saving jump, and two slender tunnels. It is no wonder why so many people died walking those miles between.

A ghost wandered here, witnessed by many unlucky enough to walk that desolate section of track on a moonless night. It would appear near Mineral City, in King Tunnel, and once in a while around Ingham Station. The spirit was described as having dark skin, eight feet tall, appearing to walk on stilts, and wearing a miner's cap with a lamp on its head and the flame flowing over his shoulders. The ghost's existence was explained as this:

24-year-old Pleasant Dexter was a coal miner and a section man for the railroad. On May 4, 1927, he left friends in Mineral City late at night and headed for home at Ingham Station. His path should have taken him a short time as it was just a couple of miles away, through King Tunnel, past King Station, and then to the house where he lived with his parents. It was a straight route, but slower than usual. He had complained earlier that his feet were aching, so he removed his shoes and padded along the wooden railroad ties into the darkness in his bare feet. But sometime during the night, he stopped to rest, lay down on the tracks, and fell asleep. During that time, three trains passed through. A man heading along the tracks discovered his broken and battered body on the west end of King Tunnel the next day. Shortly after, the ghost began to show.

LOOKOUT ROCK

Along the gravel road twisting its way past Moonville, there is a rock formation. In Ohio's early years, when the Kennedy family was settling into this area and wolves still roamed the land, they took shelter there from a pack, lighting fires to keep them at bay.

DEVIL'S TEA TABLE

There is an old legend associated with a rock formation just over the Vinton County line into Athens County. Here is a warning—do not go there on Halloween and peer from the roadway through the trees to this unique rock caused by erosion. It was once said that on midnight on Halloween, the devil dances on top. If you see him and he looks you in the eyes, he will steal your soul!

We learn that a man returning from a grocery near Moonville, in this county to his home, fell from a railroad bridge which he, attempted to cross and was instantly killed. The report of the catastrophe was soon spread, and the people, incensed at the grocery keeper, collected, broke into his establishment and destroyed a considerable quantity of the "ardent." He has resorted to the law for redress of grievances and the case will probably come before the Probate Court at its next session. We did not learn the name of the deceased.

McArthur Democrat., Jan 15, 1857

Brakeman on the Marietta and Cincinnati Railroad fell from the cars and was fatally injured. Due to "too free use of liquor."

McArthur Democrat, March 31, 1859

A 58 year-old fights a court battle with a local bully and takes his life—Mister Nathan Brewer, an old and well-known citizen of our county, committed suicide near Sand Station—About two months since he made complaint against David Keeton, one of his neighbors—

Vinton Record, March 4, 1868

Conductor Gallagher's Accommodation, on the M. & C. road east Monday morning at about half-past 6 o'clock when nearing Moonville Station collided with a freight train. A brakeman of the accommodation named McDevitt was caught between two colliding platforms and had both legs and one arm horribly mangled. McDevitt survived his injuries but a short time. No one else on either train was hurt.—The deceased we learn was about 21 years of age and leaves a widowed mother.

Athens Messenger, July 17, 1873

Thursday, October 16, 1873—While we delayed for a few minutes at Moonville on last Monday we heard reference to the instant killing of a woman in the deep cut near that town the day previous by the morning express. The name of the woman we failed to ascertain.

Athens Messenger ,October 16, 1873

Levi Sales of Moonville was run over and killed by the Fast Stock last Sunday morning. He had been at Zaleski and it was supposed he had got under the influence of liquor, laid down upon the track and gone to sleep.

Vinton Record., June 04, 1874

There was a smash-up of two freight trains at Moonville, on Tuesday, by which eleven cars were wrecked and a fireman killed, whose name we did not learn.

Vinton Record., July 16, 1874

The McArthur Enquirer, of last week, says: As we go to press this (Thursday) afternoon we learn that Henry Shirkey, the youngest son of John Shirkey, of Vinton Station, was severely injured by jumping from a box car of a freight train going West about one-fourth of a mile west of Vinton Station, at a quarter past 4 o'clock on Wednesday evening, and died 20 minutes before 6 o'clock this (Thursday) morning.

Athens Messenger, February 17, 1876

A woman named Moriarty met with a horrible death by burning, on Saturday, near Rew Station on the M. & C. road, a short distance from Moonville. While engaged at burning brush she was taken with an apoplectic fit and falling backward in the fire was almost wholly consumed before her situation was discovered.

Athens Messenger, April 13, 1876

James Hood, aged about thirty, a resident of Zaleski, while returning from Athens on the fast line on Friday, attempted to jump off the train one quarter mile east of the depot, and opposite his home. In doing so he was thrown about twenty feet against a post, and his neck broken. He has been in the habit of jumping off trains at this point in order to save walking back from the depot. He leaves a wife and three children.

Athens Messenger, May 20, 1880

Frank Lawhead, Engineer Killed in Train Wreck Near King's station in this county on Thursday last. Engineer Lawhead and Charles Krick, fireman, both of Chillicothe, were instantly killed by collision of freight trains, which, we are told, was the result of a mistake of train dispatcher. The trains were totally wrecked. . .
Athens Messenger, November 11, 1880

Michael Molboro is killed on the Marietta and Cincinnati Line. Eight years later his brother, Thomas, a brakeman is killed on the same track.
Vinton Record, February 14, 1884

A second fatality was noted in the Steubenville Weekly newspaper in January of Mrs. Mary Shea, of Moonville, aged 80, fatally hurt by a train. Mrs. Patrick Shea (in her eighties and a grandmother of Michael Shea) was walking the Moonville to Hope and while crossing the trestle was struck by a train. Her leg had to be amputated and she died from the shock. **Steubenville Weekly Herald, January 10, 1890**

The funeral train over the Baltimore and Ohio Railroad conveying to Little Hocking for burial the remains of William Chambers, who was killed in the wreck at Roxabel, struck an old woman named Deborah Allen at Moonville and she was instantly killed.
Delphos Weekly Herald, Nov 17 1892

The death of Clifton Coe occurred on Thursday evening of last week at his home at Moonville, Vinton county, just west of Mineral. Death occurred suddenly while sitting on the platform at the Moonville depot. He was sitting on the platform talking to some of his friends, when like a flash an intense pain seemed to catch him in the region of his heart, he uttered a groan of anguish and fell backward on the platform. . .

Athens Messenger and Herald, May 4, 1899

Charles Ferguson—The west bound B & O. S.-W. morning freight through here on Sunday morning killed an old man at Moonville, Athens county. The train broke at Moonville and the old man, whose name as not been learned here, attempted to cross between the sections, resulting in his death.

Chillicothe Gazette, June 16, 1902

Luhrig, O., Sept. 4.—The badly mangled body of Allen Albaugh, a middle aged miner of this place, was found under some underbrush near Moonville Saturday. Albaugh, accompanied by his brother got on a passing train and started for Zaleski. It is supposed that he staid on the train until a tunnel was reached, and that he was knocked off in some manner. When the body was found, one hand was cut off. Search was made for the missing man but not until a week later was the body found.

Athens Messenger & Herald, Sept 1907

17-year-old Raymond Burritt was killed in an explosion at a mine near Moonville February, 3, 1921

Body of Ingham Man Found in Mineral Tunnel Believed Killed By Passing Bound O Train Early in Morning. The dead body of Pleasant Dexter, 24, Inghams was found early yesterday morning in the west end of the B & O tunnel west of Mineral. . . Coroner Jones expressed the opinion this morning that the death must have occurred between 11 and 2 o'clock yesterday morning. Three trains passed west during that period. Some of the residents of the community believe Dexter went to asleep on the track. . .
Athens Messenger, May 5, 1927

Vinton Man Is Killed by Train Amzy Kennard Dies Instantly When Struck at Moonville Crossing Sunday NEW MARSHFIELD Amzy E Kennard, age 72, was instantly killed when struck by Baltimore and Ohio Train No, 3, at the Moonville Crossing near his home in Vinton County at 11:00 a.m. Sunday--
Athens Messenger, May 11, 1936

1938 Charles Landrum, Engineer Killed in Train Wreck—A heavily loaded Baltimore & Ohio Railway double-header freight train crashed into a fall of rock at 11:57 p.m. Monday night killing the engineer on one of its two engines. The mishap occurred six miles east of Zaleski between Hope and Moonville. . .The Portsmouth Times, December 27, 1938

George Gilpin. . .injured Saturday morning in an accident on a bridge construction job at Moonville, died. . . The victim was struck by a load of ties he was lifting, and was pinned against the-side of a flat car.
Athens Messenger, October 15, 1945

A 13-year-old Columbus girl died in a fall from a railroad trestle Saturday in Vinton County near Zaleski. . . was on a hiking trip with a minister and three other children when she fell from a trestle of the Moonville tunnel of the C&O Railroad. A spokesman from the Vinton County Sheriff's Department said the girl fell while a train was passing over the trestle.
Chillicothe Gazette, July 10, 1978

Visit the Ghostly Places

Path of White Thing
Infirmary Road/Powder
Plant Road
Zaleski, Ohio 45698
39.275497, -82.413221
To 39.272864, -82.4432

Hope Furnace
Lake Hope State Park
27331 OH-278
McArthur, Ohio 45651
Parking:
39.331683, -82.340234

Hope Furnace Town
Lake Hope State Park
27331 OH-278
McArthur, Ohio 45651
Parking: 39.331683,
-82.340234
Trail begins across road.

Hope Furnace Station
Moonville Rail Trail
Wheelabout Road
McArthur, Ohio 45651
39.317339, -82.351269
to 39.315995, -82.3326

Site of Train Wreck
Rail Trail by Hope-
Moonville Road
McArthur, Ohio 45651
39.312348, -82.329167

Moonville & Tunnel
Hope-Moonville Road
39.308989, -82.324775

Visit the Ghostly Places

Ingham Station
Moonville Rail Trail
Along Moonville Rail
Trail
39.308744, -82.304565

Mineral to Ingham
Kings Station & Tunnel
1157 Kings Hollow Trail
New Marshfield, Ohio
45766
Moonville Trailhead in
Mineral:
39.324745, -82.265541
to about
39.315314, -82.293982

Mineral to King Tunnel
39.324745, -82.265541
to 39.321244, -82.28028

Lookout Rock
Township Highway 1
New Marshfield, Ohio
45766
39.301711, -82.319914

The Devil's Tea Table
Township Hwy 21
(Kings Hollow Trail)
Nelsonville, Ohio 45764
39.327041, -82.270623

Citations:

Much of the core information about the towns and its peoples along with the folklore was collected from Bill Price in his interviews in the late 1950s when he was an Ohio State Park Naturalist. Part of his job was to research and collect everything he could of the town and its past. Without this research, we would know very little about the communities around Lake Hope State Park. As folklore goes, there have been many different versions of the ghosts in the communities. I used the most common version of the story substantiated, when available, by events which occurred.

Other notables:

-Philadelphia Inquirer October 14, 1889: Spooks and Spirits

-Vinton County Historical Society and Genealogical Society

-Athens Sunday Messenger November 10, 1963 newspaper

-Athens Messenger 10/10/1963 Believe in the Supernatural?

-Athens Sunday Messenger 3/11/1923

-Republican Enquirer. (McArthur, Ohio) March 29, 1920. Vinton County. 114 Years Ago in Vinton County HistoryGrabb, John R.
The Marietta & Cincinnati railroad and its successor, the Baltimore & Ohio: a study of this once great route across Ohio, 1851-1988.

-An interviews by Rich Dahn for a report in college.

-Year: 1920; Census Place: Chillicothe Ward 2, Ross, Ohio; Roll: T625_1431; Page: 15A; Enumeration District: 136

-Athens Sunday Messenger August 27, 1972

-Kathy Simcox, Historian. Interview with Clyde Pinney conducted by Kathy Simcox on Feb 23 2003

-My own conversations with locals I bump elbows with at the grocery store, school sports, work, and hiking around. The roots are deep in Vinton and Athens County and much of the folklore has been passed down and generously shared with me.
-Hope iron furnace schoolhouse. (n.d.). Retrieved from www.oldeforester.com/Hopeschs.htm
-Ferguson: familysearch.org/tree/pedigree/landscape/M2NP-GQP
-.familysearch.org/tree/pedigree/landscape/KH9G-MWD
Coes: https://www.familysearch.org/tree/pedigree/landscape/K8HJ-9J1
-findagrave.com/memorial/143566074/
-familysearch.org/tree/pedigree/landscape/996N-NXV
-Lawhead: .familysearch.org/ark:/61903/1:1:M8SK-4ZD
-George Tolliver, Moonville Ghost. Letter to Editor